NENA: THE GREEN JUICE

First published in 2020 by
Hewitt House Publishing
www.hewitthousepublishing.com

ISBN 978-1-5272-7727-4

For all enquiries email: info@hewitthousepublishing.com

H
-
H

HEWITT
HOUSE
PUBLISHING

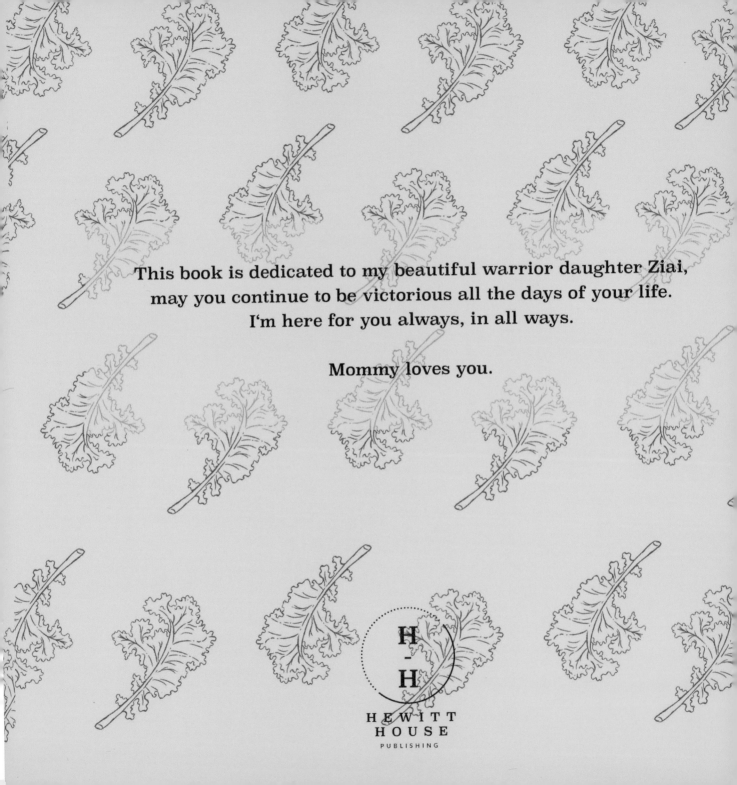

This book is dedicated to my beautiful warrior daughter Ziai,
may you continue to be victorious all the days of your life.
I'm here for you always, in all ways.

Mommy loves you.

H
-
H
HEWITT
HOUSE
PUBLISHING

It was a hot day when Mommy, Nena and Melly were in the garden hanging out clothes on the washing line.

"I'm so thirsty!' said Nena, wiping the sweat off her forehead.
"Okay, let's go and make some green juice," said Mommy.
"Green juice? Mommy, what's that?" Nena said with a puzzled look on her face.

"Just follow me and you will see,"
said Mommy. Nena and Melly excitedly
followed Mommy into the kitchen.

Mommy took lots of vegetables out of the fridge and got a big silver shiny machine out of the cupboard.

"**What's that?**" said Nena pointing to the **strange** looking machine. "It's a juicer," said Mommy. "Doooser?" said Melly. "Yes, juicer Melly, aren't you a clever girl!" said Mommy.

"What's it used for?" asked Nena.
"It's used to get the juice out of fruits
and vegetables," said Mommy.

Nena started laughing,
"Oh Mommy,
**vegetables don't
have juice!**
We can't drink them!"

"Oh yes they do, Nena, watch and see. Don't just stand there, come and help me," said Mommy.

"The first thing we are going to put into the juicer is a carrot," said Mommy.

Nena looked confused,
"A carrot?"
she said. "Yes, a carrot!
Carrots are really good for
helping your eyes, skin
and hair," said Mommy.

Mommy chopped up the chunky carrot and handed the pieces to Nena and Melly. They put the pieces inside the juicer and Mommy pressed the "on" button. It made a **loud buzzing** sound and the carrot turned into liquid.

"Oh my gosh, it's watery!" said Nena in surprise,
"but it's not green Mommy, it's orange."

"Patience Nena. Patience," said Mommy.

Mommy then picked up a round red vegetable. "This is a beetroot; it's really good for helping the blood flow around our bodies. Beetroot grows in the ground" said Mommy.

Mommy chopped up the round red beetroot and handed the pieces to Nena and Melly. They put the pieces inside the juicer and Mommy pressed the "on" button. It made a **loud buzzing** sound and the beetroot turned into liquid.

"**WOW**!" said Nena surprised, "but it's not green Mommy, it's red."

"Just you wait and see," said Mommy.

Mommy then picked up a long green vegetable. "This is a cucumber; it's really good for helping our brain memory. Cucumbers grow on a vine," said Mommy.

Mommy chopped up the long green cucumber and handed the pieces to Nena and Melly. They put the pieces inside the juicer and Mommy pressed the "on" button. It made a **loud buzzing** sound and the cucumber turned into liquid. Nena looked at the liquid. **"It's not green Mommy. It's still red,"** she said.

"Soon Nena, soon," Mommy said smiling.

Mommy then picked up an apple.
"Apple keeps our hearts healthy and will
also make the juice nice and sweet.
This apple grew on Nanny's tree
in her garden," said Mommy.

Mommy chopped up the big red apple and handed the pieces to Nena and Melly. They put the pieces inside the juicer and Mommy pressed the "on" button. It made a **loud buzzing** sound. "The apple has turned into liquid," said Nena, "but it's not green, Mommy, now it's brown. **It's never going to turn green!**"

"You will soon see, Nena," said Mommy.

Mommy picked up some big green leaves. "Now it's time for the special ingredient, this is kale," said Mommy, "Kale is a powerful vegetable; it helps our liver, kidneys and brain to function. It also gives us lots of energy." Mommy chopped up the big green leaves and handed the pieces to Nena and Melly. They put the pieces inside the juicer and Mommy pressed the "on" button. It made a **loud buzzing** sound and the kale turned into liquid.

"Wow, Mommy! The juice has turned green! **Now it's green juice,**" said Nena. Mommy put the green juice into cups and they all drank it together.

"This tastes yummy, Mommy.
I love green juice,"
said Nena, licking her lips.

Printed in Poland
by Amazon Fulfillment
Poland Sp. z o.o., Wrocław

67628373R00016